EXTREME WEATHER JOBS



# STORM CHASERS

BY DALTON RAINS

WWW.APEXEDITIONS.COM



Apex is distributed by North Star Editions:
sales@northstareditions.com | 888-417-0195

Produced for Apex by Red Line Editorial.

Photographs ©: Ryan McGinnis/Alamy, cover; iStockphoto, 1, 14–15, 20–21, 22–23; Sue Ogrocki/AP Images, 4–5; NWS/NOAA, 6; Shutterstock Images, 7, 8–9; Ryan McGinnis/Moment/Getty Images, 10–11, 18; Orlin Wagner/AP Images, 12; Jim Reed Photography/Science Source, 13, 16–17, 27, 29; Kim Shiflett/NASA, 24–25

**Library of Congress Control Number: 2023922218**

**ISBN**
978-1-63738-920-1 (hardcover)
978-1-63738-960-7 (paperback)
979-8-89250-056-2 (ebook pdf)
979-8-89250-018-0 (hosted ebook)

Printed in the United States of America
Mankato, MN
082024

## NOTE TO PARENTS AND EDUCATORS

**Apex books are designed to build literacy skills in striving readers. Exciting, high-interest content attracts and holds readers' attention. The text is carefully leveled to allow students to achieve success quickly. Additional features, such as bolded glossary words for difficult terms, help build comprehension.**

# TABLE OF CONTENTS

CHAPTER 1

# TRACKING TORNADOES

A pickup truck races down a highway. Three storm chasers sit inside. One person drives. The others watch computer screens. They use **radar** to track nearby clouds.

**If a large storm is forming, many storm chasers may rush to an area.**

# CLOUD SHAPES

Storm chasers watch clouds for signs of severe weather. Supercells are one example. These thunderstorms have tall, swirling clouds. Their spinning wind can cause **tornadoes**.

Hook echoes are curved shapes that show up on radar. They can be signs of spinning wind.

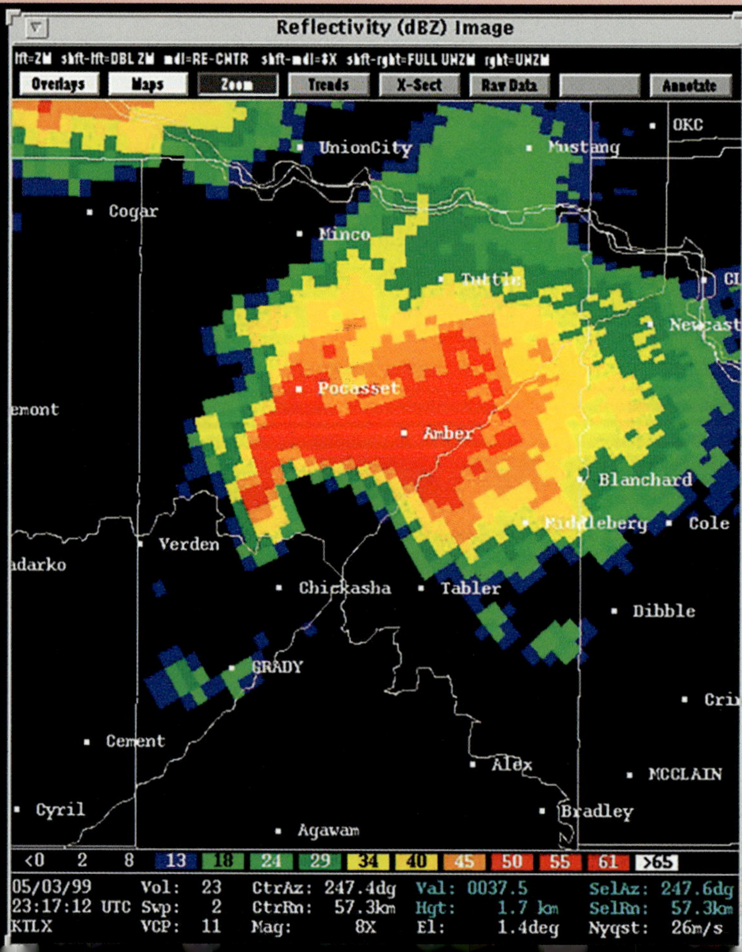

A tornado forms. The storm chasers take pictures of it. They measure the wind speed and air temperature, too.

About 20 percent of supercell thunderstorms create tornadoes.

## FAST FACT

Some tornado winds are faster than 200 miles per hour (322 km/h).

CHAPTER 2

# HISTORY

Storm chasing began in the 1950s and 1960s. People listened to weather reports on their car radios. Then they drove toward storms.

Driving toward storms is very risky. Storm chasers can be hurt or killed.

At first, storm chasing was just a hobby. But by the 1970s, chasers often worked with scientists. They helped people learn about how storms formed.

Up-close views from storm chasers' cameras helped scientists understand storms.

The National Severe Storms Laboratory has been researching storms since the 1960s.

## EARLY WORK

David Hoadley was one of the first storm chasers. He chased storms as a hobby. Neil Ward was the first person to chase storms for research.

In the 2000s, many storm chasers began using the internet. They could share more **data**. That way, they could more easily find and follow storms.

Today, many storm chasers use computers to track the size and location of storms.

## FAST FACT

The movie *Twister* came out in 1996. It showed storm chasers. It inspired many people to try chasing.

CHAPTER 3

# WHAT IT TAKES

Few people chase storms as a full-time job. But all chasers need training and practice. Many storm chasers study meteorology. They learn about storms and how they form.

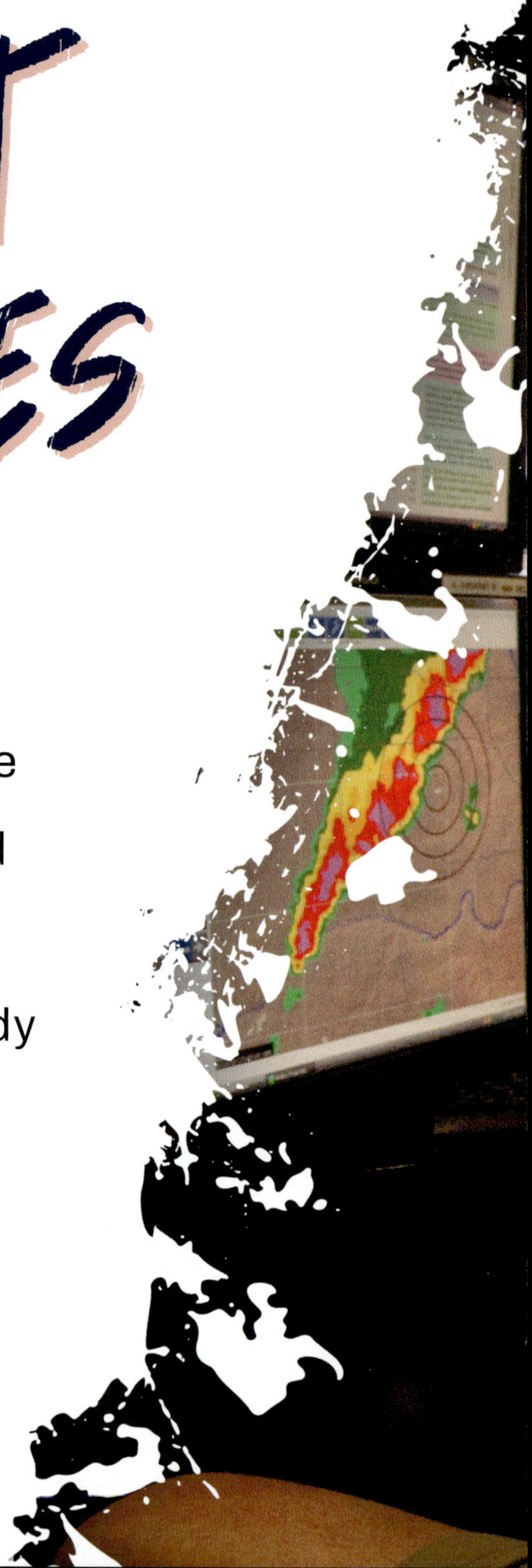

Chasers learn to watch for common causes of storms, such as sudden changes in air temperature.

Storm chasers also need vehicles. Some drive trucks or cars. Others use armored vehicles. These vehicles have extra-thick sides. They help chasers stay safe.

## DRIVING DANGERS

Driving near storms is risky. Wet roads can be slippery. Wind can blow **debris**. Lightning and hail are dangers, too. But the biggest risk is other vehicles. Drivers must take care not to crash.

◀ Armored vehicles have thick metal layers added to their sides.

FAST FACT
Some chasers put **antennas** on their vehicles.

Measuring wind speed, rain, and air pressure can show how bad a storm will be.

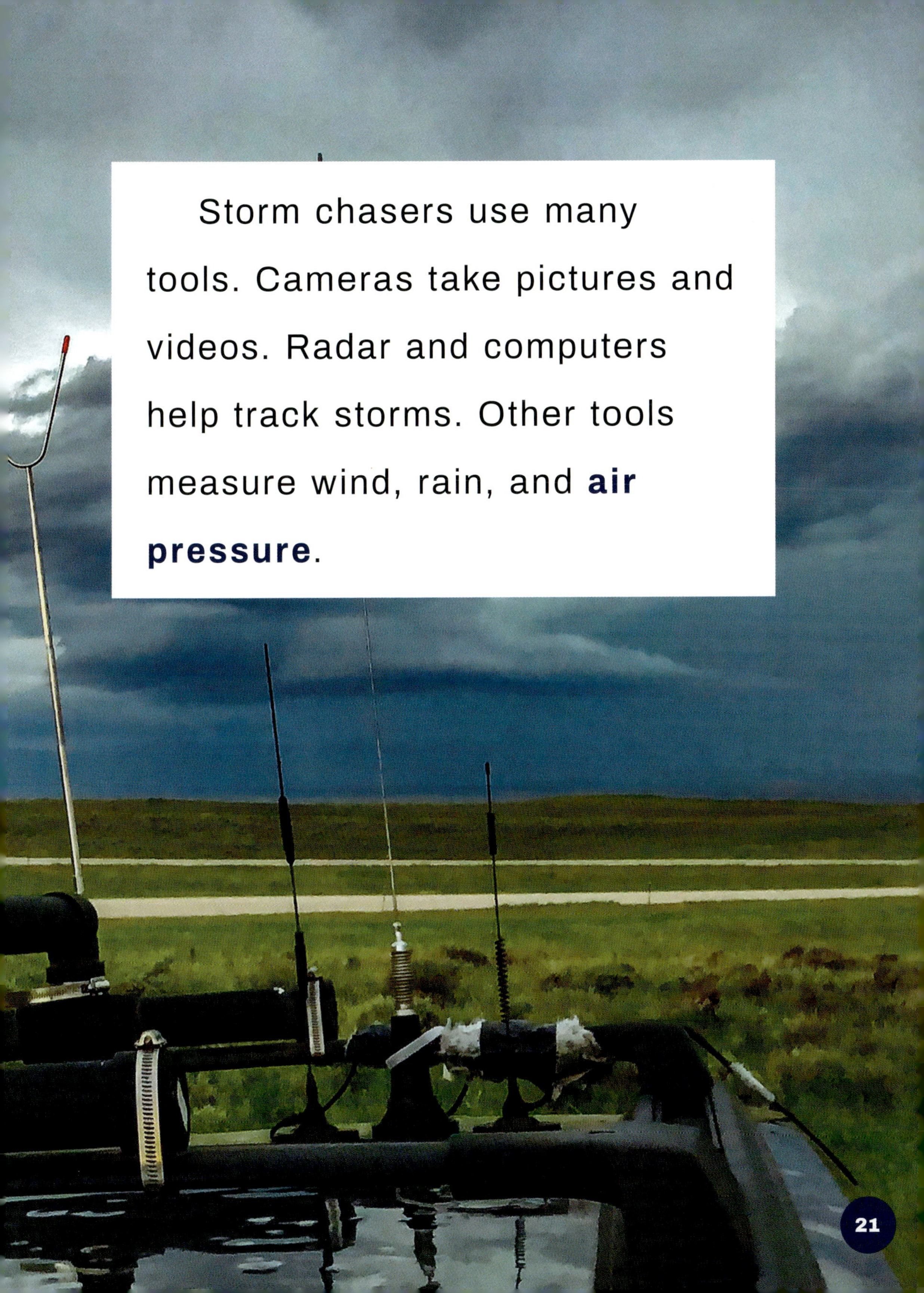

Storm chasers use many tools. Cameras take pictures and videos. Radar and computers help track storms. Other tools measure wind, rain, and **air pressure**.

CHAPTER 4

# ON THE JOB

Storm chasers spend most of their time away from storms. They do lots of planning. First, they figure out where storms are likely. Then they drive to those places.

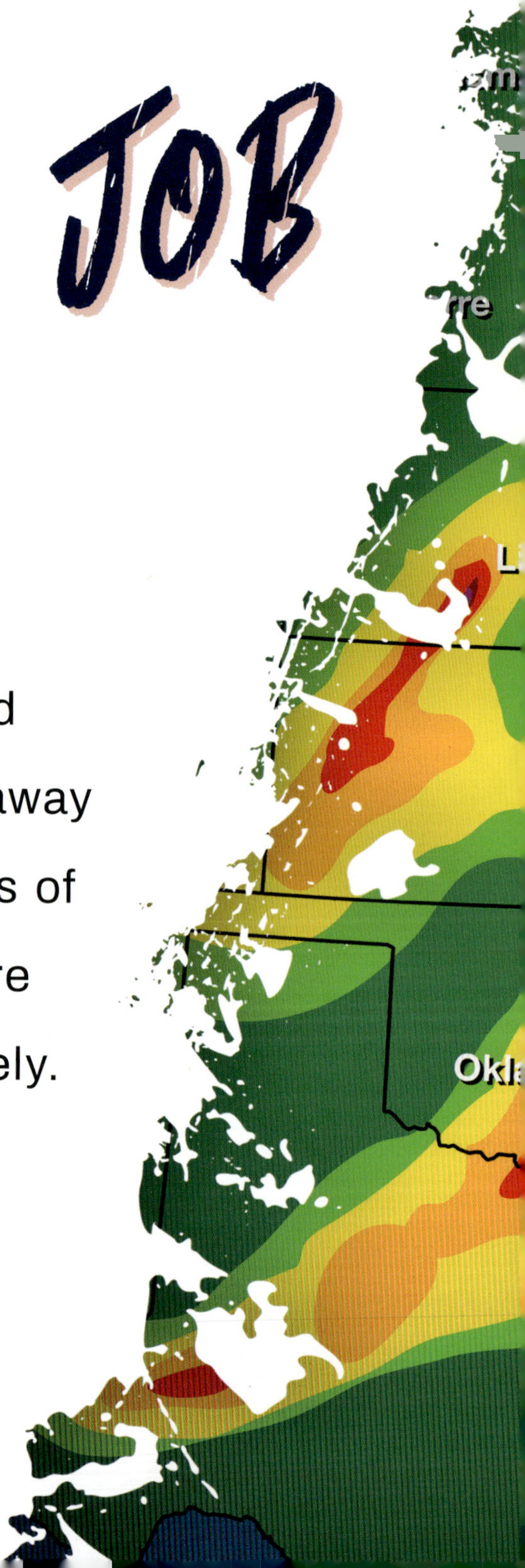

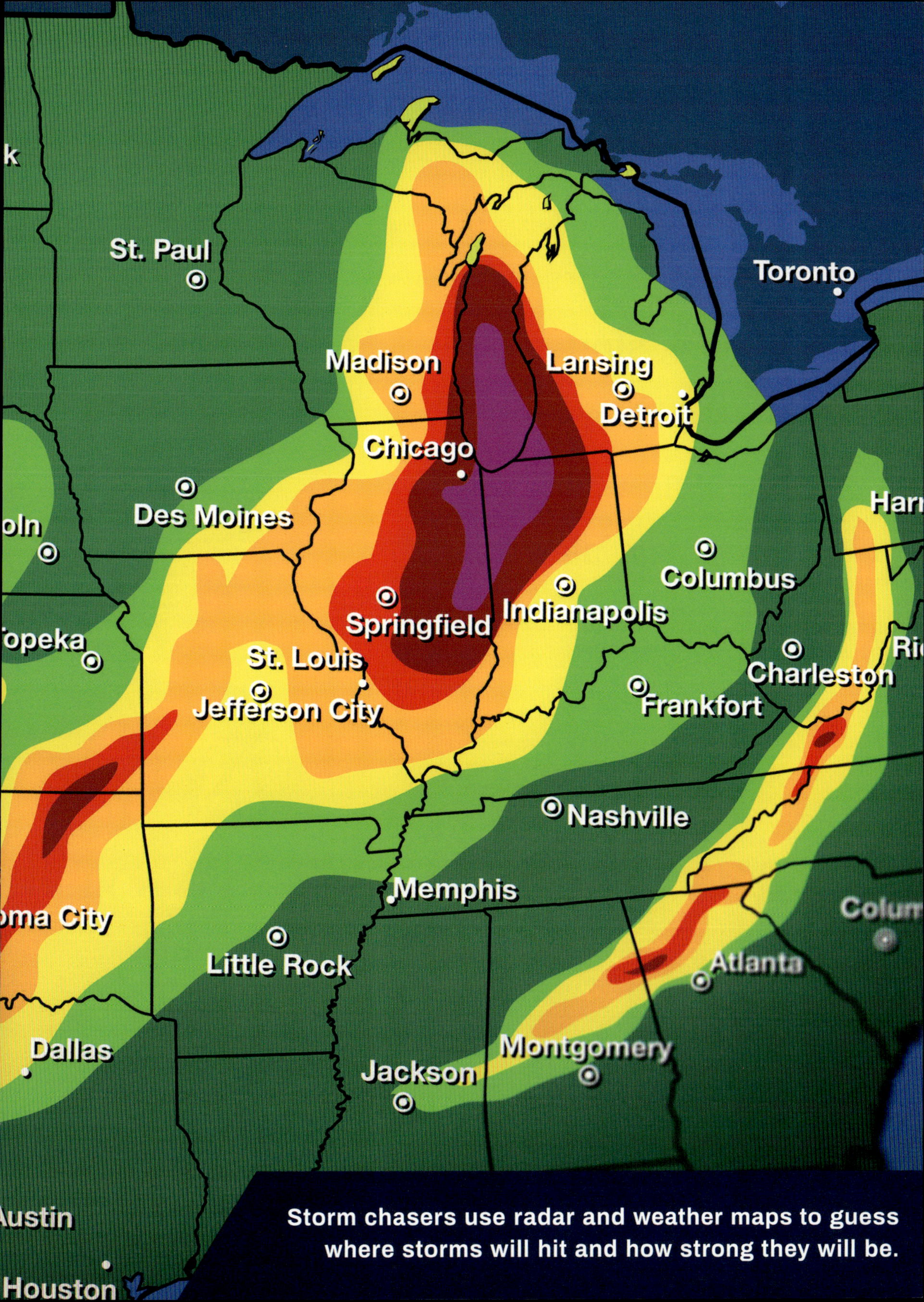


Storm chasers use radar and weather maps to guess where storms will hit and how strong they will be.

People may drive for many hours before reaching storms. Along the way, they keep collecting data. This helps them plan their route.

## FAST FACT

Some storm chasers release weather balloons. These balloons rise high into the air and collect information.

Weather balloons measure the air's pressure and temperature at different heights.

Some storm chasers find thunderstorms or tornadoes. Others follow hurricanes. Many share their data with scientists. They help people understand and prepare for storms.

## WARNING OTHERS

Tornadoes are hard to **predict**. Scientists are still learning how and why they form. Gathering data helps them make better guesses. That way, they can send warnings and help people stay safe.

Some trucks carry radar. They help scientists map and study storms.

# COMPREHENSION QUESTIONS

*Write your answers on a separate piece of paper.*

1. Write a few sentences describing the main ideas of Chapter 2.

2. What fact about storm chasers was most surprising to you? Why?

3. When did storm chasing first start?

   A. the 1950s
   B. the 1970s
   C. the 2000s

4. How does having more data help scientists make better guesses?

   A. They can find common patterns.
   B. They can ignore facts from the past.
   C. They can stop sending warnings.

**5.** What does **meteorology** mean in this book?

*Many storm chasers study **meteorology**. They learn about storms and how they form.*

**A.** the study of long-ago times
**B.** the study of outer space
**C.** the study of weather

**6.** What does **risk** mean in this book?

*Lightning and hail are dangers, too. But the biggest **risk** is other vehicles.*

**A.** type of weather
**B.** cause of danger
**C.** way to stay safe

*Answer key on page 32.*

# GLOSSARY

**air pressure**

The force of air pushing down on Earth. Changes in pressure often lead to changes in weather.

**antennas**

Long rods or wires that send or pick up information.

**data**

Information collected to study or track something.

**debris**

Pieces of something that broke or fell apart.

**predict**

To guess what will happen in the future.

**radar**

A system that uses radio waves to find the position or speed of something.

**tornadoes**

Storms with strong, spinning winds that stretch down from thunderstorms and touch the ground.

# TO LEARN MORE

## BOOKS

Murray, Julie. *Storm Chasers*. Minneapolis: Abdo Publishing, 2021.

Rathburn, Betsy. *Hurricanes*. Minneapolis: Bellwether Media, 2020.

Rossiter, Brienna. *Tornadoes*. Mendota Heights, MN: Apex Editions, 2023.

## ONLINE RESOURCES

Visit **www.apexeditions.com** to find links and resources related to this title.

## ABOUT THE AUTHOR

Dalton Rains is a writer and editor who lives in Minnesota.

# INDEX



**ANSWER KEY:**
1. Answers will vary; 2. Answers will vary; 3. A; 4. A; 5. C; 6. B